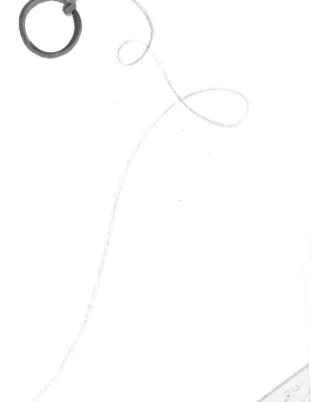

Library of Congress Cataloging-in-Publication Data

Edwards, Pamela Duncan.
Dinosaur starts school / by Pamela Duncan Edwards ;
illustrated by Deborah Allwright.
p. cm.
Summary: Dinosaur doesn't think going to school is such a great idea,
but with the help of some gentle advice, he finds that he has fun.
ISBN 978-0-8075-1600-3
[1. Dinosaurs—Fiction. 2. First day of school—Fiction. 3. Worry—Fiction.]
I. Allwright, Deborah, ill. II. Title.
PZ7.E26365Dk 2009 [E]—dc22 2008031708

First published in Great Britain in 2008
by Macmillan Children's Books.

For more information about Albert Whitman & Company,
visit our web site at www.albertwhitman.com.

For Margaret and David Minch
and all those wonderful
grandchildren,
with love P.D.E.

For Pablo and Oscar,
with love D.A.

Pamela Duncan Edwards

Dinosaur
Starts School

illustrated by
Deborah Allwright

ALBERT WHITMAN & COMPANY
Morton Grove, Illinois

What would you do if on the very first day of school Dinosaur wasn't smiling his **big, toothy** dinosaur smile?

You'd say, "Don't worry, Dinosaur.
School will be **fun!**"

What if he **stamped** his feet

and **roared** in his
loudest dinosaur voice,

RROOARR!

"But dinosaurs don't
have to go to school!"

You'd say, "Of course they do, Dinosaur. Otherwise, how would dinosaurs grow up to be so smart?"

What if you got to the school gates, but Dinosaur
wrapped his sharp claws around the fence
and said in his timid dinosaur voice,
"But it's too **big.** I'll get lost."

You'd say, "Don't be silly!
You can't get lost because our classroom
is just the right size for dinosaurs."

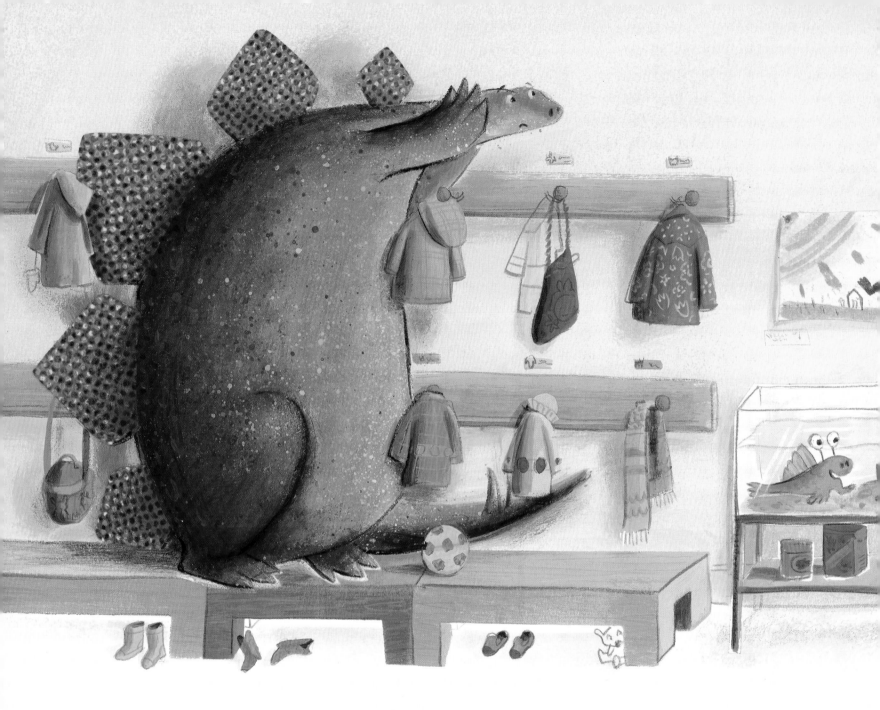

What if you reached the classroom door but Dinosaur covered his tiny ears and said in his quiet dinosaur voice, "But it's too NOISY. I'll get a headache."

You'd say, "It's only noisy because everyone is laughing and having a good time."

What if the teacher asked all
the children to say their names?

What if Dinosaur turned away and
tried to hide under the table?

You'd say, "I think you should tell the teacher your name, Dinosaur. She might think you're not here and give someone else your crayons by mistake."

What if you were painting
pictures of the sun but Dinosaur
made a big mess?

What if his bright dinosaur eyes filled
with tears and he began to cry?

You'd say, "Wow, Dinosaur! You've made sunbeams
come out of your sun. I wish I'd thought of that."

What if it was time for lunch but Dinosaur said in his worried dinosaur voice, "They might give us something yucky to eat."

You'd say, "We'll tell them that some dinosaurs are herbivores and don't like meat. Then you can have salad instead of hot dogs."

What if everyone ran out to play but Dinosaur hid behind you and looked shy?

What if you and Dinosaur noticed someone else looking shy, too?

I bet Dinosaur would whisper in his gentlest dinosaur voice,
"Want to play on the swings together?"

Then you and Dinosaur and your new friend would have a great time pushing each other on the swings.

You'd take turns on the seesaw.

You'd build a castle in the sandbox.

You'd play tag until you
were giggling so hard you
couldn't run anymore.

What if at the end of the day you said, "I told you school was fun, Dinosaur. Shall we come back again tomorrow?"

I bet he'd nod his handsome dinosaur head.

Then I bet he'd smile his
big, toothy dinosaur smile.

And I bet that you'd
smile right back.

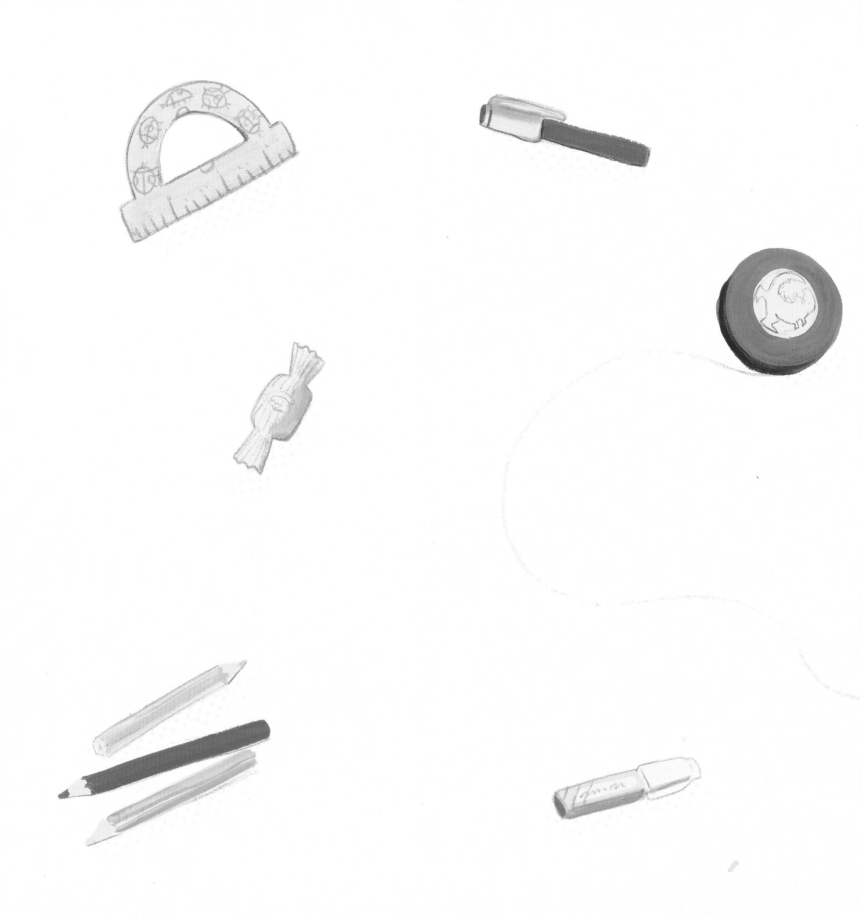